I0784065

ANNA

and the

JEWEL THIEVES

ANNA

and the

JEWEL THIEVES

MORTIMER TUNE

ILLUSTRATIONS BY DAVID KELLEY

First Published in Great Briatain by Black Apollo Press, 1998

New edition by Petite Germinal, 2015

ISBN: 9781906448417

A Petite Germinal book
Germinal Productions, Ltd
www.germinalproductions.com
Cambridge, UK

en famille

Chapter One

MR AND MRS Marple of Prairieview, Iowa, and their ten-year-old daughter, Anna, were about to take their first trip abroad, though they didn't know it yet.

Mr Marple had a small business manufacturing tea cosies – those cute, little knitted pullovers for tea pots – but the Iowa tea cosy market had been rather sluggish of late and the future of this furry device which had done so much to help thousands of chipped ceramic vessels keep warm on cold midwestern nights was somewhat less than optimistic. In fact, Mr Marple's financial situation looked very grim.

Then, one day, he received a letter which read: "Dear Mr Marple, we heard you were having some difficulties paying your bills. Here is a credit card to help you out. With it you can charge your purchases and then pay them off slowly. Buy anything, go anywhere you like. Have a good time! Yours truly, The Bank."

"Fine," said Mrs Marple, when her husband showed her the Bank's letter. "Let's go to Europe!"

"Go to Europe? Are you crazy? We're going bankrupt!" Mr Marple shouted at his wife, though he regretted his rudeness a moment later.

"Then this will be our last chance, won't it?" said Mrs Marple with some logic. "Certainly we can manage four or five days abroad. Besides, with this new credit card we might as well go now, while our business is off, and pay our bills later, when things begin to improve for us."

"Maybe you have a point," Mr Marple agreed. "Which country would you like to visit?"

"Well," replied Mrs Marple, tapping a finger on her chubby cheek, "I've always wanted to go to England to visit the Queen. Perhaps we could even convince her to buy some of our tea cosies. I hear the English drink a lot of tea."

"All right," said Mr Marple, beginning to feel the thrill of impending adventure (for, in fact, he had always wanted to go to some strange and far-off country, and the thought of combining it with a business trip seemed to make perfect sense). "I'll call the travel agent."

"And France to see the Eiffel Tower..." Mrs Marple continued.

"Both England and France?" Mr Marple said, quickly revising the imagined itinerary in his mind. "Don't you think that's a bit too much for an extended weekend?"

"And Italy to see the Spanish Steps..."

"All in five days?" asked Mr Marple. And then scratching his balding head he added, "Aren't the Spanish Steps in Spain?"

Mrs Marple answered her husband's question patiently. "We can't afford any more than five days even with a credit card, but if we plan our trip with the same efficiency we use to run our business then I'm sure we can manage three small countries in that length of time. As for the Spanish Steps, they are in Rome which is a city in Italy. And it is because of these serious gaps in your education that our daughter, Anna, must be given the chance to see the world, lest she end up as provincial as her father."

Mr Marple nodded his head in agreement because he knew, down deep, that what his wife said was true. His geography was very poor and he had never travelled further than Council Bluffs, a mere twenty minutes from his hometown of Prairieview.

And so, on a moderately warm Saturday, the 5th of May, at six o'clock in the morning, Mr and Mrs Marple and Anna, found themselves flying several thousand feet over the Atlantic Ocean on their way to London. If they had known the strange adventures which lay in store for them, it is possible they would have tried to convince the pilot to swing the plane around in the sky and turn back.

Chapter Two

ONE OF THE less commonly known items from the Manual of Royal Housekeeping is that every other Saturday of the month the Queen's jewels are sent out for a good scrubbing, waxing and polishing. Traditionally, this job was done by the Palace itself, but due to necessary cost-cutting measures, it was now being farmed out to a little shop in North London called Mary's Café and Diamond Cleaner's.

Mary's is one of the few cafés left where you can read the morning paper, eat a breakfast of sausage, eggs and grilled tomatoes (kippers on Friday), while getting your diamonds cleaned all at the same time. And be you royalty or just an ordinary, everyday person, you can be assured of the same exceptional standard of service (though the fried bread may leave something to be desired).

Each alternate Saturday, Mary herself drives up to Buckingham Palace to collect all the jewellery in need of cleaning. She comes alone in the very early hours of the morning, driving a little red Mini which she parks by the front entrance. Then she toots her horn three times (though very quietly so as not to wake the Queen). That is the signal for the butler to bring out the jewels.

The jewels are packed in little velvet bags tied securely with a lavender ribbon and are carried out on a silver tray. Mary takes these little bags of jewels and puts them in the back of her car next to the sausages she has just picked up from the wholesale butcher (not out of disrespect, mind you, but simply because the car is so tiny). Then she drives back to North London where the jewels will be polished in a small room off the kitchen while the sausages are being grilled for all the patrons who had brought in their own jewels for cleaning and are waiting for their breakfasts to be served.

Now, also in London, there lived a gang of misfits who were training to be thieves. The head of the gang was Fat Al who really was fat and smoked cheap cigars besides. The second in command was Little Albert, who was quite short and tried very hard to look like Fat Al, whom he much admired, by wearing the same cloth cap Fat Al had once worn (even though it came down over his eyes) and sticking out his tummy. Finally there was Henry-the-Nose who was tall and thin and wore thick glasses over his sleepy eyes and had a great, big, red schnozz that was very sensitive to the touch. Henry was a little dim, but he could also be quite loveable.

Before they had decided to become thieves, the three of them had been musicians. Little Albert had played an old, beat-up banjo, Fat Al had played a triangle (which made a little dinging sound when he tapped it with a thin glass rod), and Henry-the-Nose had played a used bicycle horn which he had found in a rubbish bin. The height of their musical career was several months before when they had played to a crowd of thousands underneath Piccadilly Circus in one of the tunnels leading to the Bakerloo line. Unfortunately, when they divided the day's takings collected in Fat Al's cap, they only found three American pennies, a strange Japanese coin with a hole in it and twenty-five metal rings from the tops of soft drink cans.

The idea came to them one morning just before a concert they were to give deep under Leicester Square when they had stopped for tea at Mary's.

"Three milky teas," Fat Al had said when Mary came over to their table, holding a little notebook and a pencil which she used to take down the orders.

"Right you are, luv," said Mary. "No sausages or fried bread today?"

"No," said Fat Al, who really would have loved some sausages and fried bread, but couldn't afford it. "I'm on a diet," he explained.

"Everyone's on a diet these days," said Mary in a commiserating sort of voice. And then, turning to Little Albert and Henry-the-Nose, she looked at them inquisitively and said, "How about you lads?"

"We'll have three milky teas, too," said Little Albert, who always ordered the same thing as Fat Al.

"So that'll be nine milky teas then?" asked Mary.

"I just want three," said Henry-the-Nose.

Mary scribbled down the order and then, as an afterthought, she said, "No diamonds that need cleaning or polishing today?"

"Not today," said Fat Al.

"Oi!" said Henry-the-Nose. "Do we look like we 'ave diamonds 'at need cleaning?"

"No," said Mary. "I used to know right away if a customer wanted their diamonds cleaned or just a quick sausage and egg. But not anymore. Times have changed."

"Not for us they haven't," said Little Albert looking under the table at his flappy shoes.

After Mary had gone to fill their order, Henry-the-Nose looked at his mates through his thick glasses that made his eyes as big and round as fish bowls. "Do yer suppose she really cleans diamonds 'ere?" he asked.

Fat Al gave Henry-the-Nose a look of disgust. Then he reached over and gave Henry's nose a tweak (which wasn't very nice and made Henry sneeze, but Fat Al just couldn't help himself).

"What does the sign on the window say?"asked Fat Al.

Henry-the-Nose turned around and looked at the window. "'ow should I know? It's written backwards, i'n'it?"

"Try looking at it with your head upside down," suggested Little Albert, attempting to be helpful.

Henry-the-Nose bent his head toward the floor and looked at the window again, following Little Albert's advice. "I still can't read it!" he complained.

Fat Al lit up a cheap cigar, took a puff and then closed his eyes. "The sign says 'Mary's Café and Diamond Cleaners'. Now why do you think the sign would say that if she didn't clean diamonds?"

Henry-the-Nose was still thinking this one out when Mary brought them their nine cups of tea. "Drink up, luvs," she said. And then she went away.

Little Albert plunked three cubes of sugar in each cup just like Fat Al had done, stirred each of them twice, just like Fat Al did, and drank them one by one, following Fat Al's every gesture.

Meanwhile Henry-the-Nose was still pondering the question Fat Al had asked. Finally, he blinked his wide, fish-bowl eyes and said, "I dunno, Fat Al. Why would it say 'Mary's Café and Diamond Cleaners' if she didn't clean diamonds?"

Fat Al made a face and reached across the table and tweaked Henry's nose again causing him to sneeze twelve sneezes in quick succession. "It says that because she does clean diamonds!" he replied with some exasperation.

Henry's nose lit up from his fit of sneezing and also because he had an idea. "Oi! Maybe we should steal 'em, Fat Al!"

"No," said Fat Al, "that wouldn't be right. We don't know who they belong to."

"Don't you remember our motto?" Little Albert asked Henry-the-Nose. "It's steal from the rich and give to the poor," he reminded him.

"No, you lump head!" Fat Al sighed. "That's Robin Hood's motto. Our motto is 'Steal from the rich and give to ourselves!"

"Oh, yeah," said Little Albert, suddenly recalling that they had, indeed, discussed this point before.

"And until we find out if these diamonds belong to someone very rich, we can't steal them!" said Fat Al.

The other two nodded their heads in agreement.

Fat Al took a puff on his smelly cigar and leaned forward with a mischievous smile on his face. "But let's keep our eyes open, lads. Maybe there'll be something for us at that!"

Chapter Three

FOR THE NEXT few days, Fat Al, Little Albert and Henry-the-Nose kept a watch on the café. Then, early one Saturday morning, when Mary left in her Mini, they followed on their two-man bicycle with Fat Al and Henry-the-Nose peddling like mad and Little Albert sitting on the front handle bars with his legs crossed as if he were a ship's masthead.

They followed her all the way to the wholesale butchers, where she picked up her weekly supply of sausages and then on to Buckingham Palace, where she collected the Queen's jewels. They would have continued to follow her all the way back to her café, except Henry-the-Nose insisted on stopping at Hyde Park to feed the ducks that live in the Serpentine Lake.

That evening the gang held a meeting at their flat on Plympton Road.

"OK," said Fat Al, lighting a cigar and looking at his two comrades in crime, "does anyone have any questions?"

Henry-the-Nose raised his hand.

"You don't need to raise your hand," said Fat Al.

At first Henry-the-Nose looked slightly confused. Then, after a moment's consideration, he raised his foot.

"You don't have to raise either your hand or your foot to speak," said Fat Al, starting to turn red. "Just tell us what's on your mind!"

Henry-the Nose felt the top his head. "I don't think anything is on it, but I can't see 'cause it's inside me noggin..."

"SPEAK!" Fat Al shouted.

"Is the Queen rich?" asked Henry-the-Nose.

Both Fat Al and Little Albert began to laugh. They laughed so hard that they cried. "Is she rich?" said Fat Al through his chortling. "Does a porpoise have hair?"

Henry-the-Nose thought a minute. "I dunno. Does a porpoise 'ave 'air?" He looked at Little Albert.

Little Albert stopped laughing and scratched his head. "I don't know either." He looked at Fat Al.

Fat Al's face was growing very red.

"I think 'e's angry," said Henry-the-Nose, pointing over at Fat Al.

"Yeah. Very angry," said Little Albert.

"My Mum used to get angry. Did yers?"

Little Albert shook his head. "Only when I wore my shoes to bed."

"Shut up!" shouted Fat Al at the top of his lungs and he leaned over and tweaked Henry's nose with his left hand and Little Albert's nose with his right. Which was the only way he knew to restore order, but it didn't do much to endear him to his friends.

After Henry-the-Nose stopped his fit of sneezing and quiet once more prevailed, Fat Al answered the question in a more straightforward way. "The Queen is the richest woman in all of England!" he said.

"How do you know?" asked Little Albert, who was still upset at having his nose tweaked.

"How could she afford the mortgage on that great, big palace if not? And Buckingham isn't her only palace, she's got palaces all over England and Scotland and even Wales. And every palace is filled to the top with gold and jewels. Once – and I read this in a newspaper so I know it's true

– her sink was stuffed up and she had to call a plumber.
And do you know what the plumber found jammed in the
pipe? A great, big diamond ring, that's what! She must have
taken it off when she was doing the washing up and it fell
into the drain. And she didn't even miss it!"

Chapter Four

ON THE VERY same Saturday morning that Mr and Mrs Marple and their daughter, Anna, left for England, a jewel robbery took place outside of Buckingham Palace. This is what happened:

Mary had already made her morning pickup of the little bags of dirty diamonds which, according to habit, had been placed in the back of her Mini next to the sausages. She was just driving out the front gate when a very fat man smoking a cheap cigar and riding a bicycle built for two all alone pulled alongside of her and shouted – "You got a flat in your left rear, luv!"

Of course, Mary immediately stopped the Mini to inspect the tyres. As soon as she got out, however, her attention was diverted by a short man with a cloth cap over his eyes who was standing on the pavement playing her favourite song – "The Streets of London" – on a banjo. Not stopping to think why a busker such as this would be playing his music on the deserted road next to Buckingham Palace at six AM, Mary politely waited for the song to end so she could throw a two penny piece into the young man's cap.

But as she waited for the overly long song to be completed, she failed to see the same fat man who had ridden past her on the bicycle built for two, sneak behind and open the passenger door to her Mini. Nor did she see as he quickly took each of the packages wrapped in butcher paper from the rear seat and threw them to a man with thick glasses and a bright, red nose who was hidden in the shrubs.

Fortunately for Mary, however, the thief (who was really Fat Al) had only got to the first tiny, velvet bag when the accident took place. He had thrown the little bag of jewels a bit too high in the air and Henry-the-Nose (who was the man behind the shrubs) had bobbled it, whereupon the bag of jewels had bounced onto his sniffer causing him, of course, to sneeze. The sneeze, which was a mighty one, shot the velvet bag high into the air and also caused Mary to turn around. Seeing the dastardly activity going on behind her back, Mary ran swiftly to the car, while Fat Al beat a hasty retreat into the shrubs where Henry-the-Nose was hiding.

As soon as Mary looked inside the open door of the Mini, she realised at once what had happened. "Good Lord!" she exclaimed. "All me sausages have been nicked!" And she glanced back up just in time to see Fat Al, Little Albert and Henry-the-Nose peddling off as fast as humanly possible, into the rising sun.

The Marples had arrived in London early the same day the jewel robbery had taken place at Buckingham Palace and, having checked into their bed and breakfast – a charming, little place in the Kensington district, run by a Mr Mango Muldoon, who gladly accepted their credit card – they sat down to check through the detailed itinerary that Mrs Marple had written up (after researching in her marvellous guide book, *Around the World in Seven Days, Three Hours and Fourteen Minutes*) telling them what they would do and where they would be every precious second, from dawn till dusk.

"At 2:30 PM," Mrs Marple said, "we are due at the Palace. I took the precaution of writing the Queen to tell her of the time so she could make sure to schedule us in. After all, it wouldn't have been considerate of us to drop in on her unannounced."

Mr Marple nodded his head. He was very proud of his wife's good sense. Then, glancing at his watch he said, "It's one-fifteen now, dear. Shouldn't we go?"

"Yes," said Mrs Marple, standing up to brush off her new magenta stretch slacks that she had put on especially for the occasion. "If we leave now, we'll have time to do the Tate Gallery and perhaps even one third of the British Museum." Then, turning to her daughter, who was sulking in the corner, she said, "Hurry up, Anna, dear! We don't want to keep the Queen waiting!"

"I don't want to go!" said Anna, crossly. And she squeezed her little fists very tight as angry tears filled her eyes.

"Heavens, child!" her mother said in a rebuking tone of voice. "We're doing all this for you so that when you're a mother you'll be able to tell your children about your wonderful trip abroad and how you had tea with the Queen!"

"I don't want to have tea with the Queen!" Anna persisted.

Mr Marple was quite concerned, for his daughter was turning blue in the face. "Why don't you want to have tea with the Queen, Anna?" he asked. "I'm sure she's a very polite lady and perhaps she'll even offer you a sweet..."

"I think she's abominably horrible!" Anna cried.

"For goodness' sake, why?" asked Mrs Marple, quite amazed at her child's curious vocabulary.

"Because she cuts off people's heads!" Anna replied.

"Oh, nonsense, Anna," Mrs Marple laughed. "The Queen doesn't do things like that herself. She has someone else do it for her! A Queen has much more important things to do with her time."

Mr Marple stood up. "Come on, Anna!" he said. "It's time to go!"

"I don't want to go!" Anna insisted. And she crossed her arms and looked at her father defiantly.

"What are we going to do with her?" Mrs Marple asked her husband. "After all, we can't be late for our appointment."

Mr Marple sighed. "All right, Anna," he said. "What do you want this time?"

"A bright, blue coat with a fur lining!" she said, without a moment's hesitation.

"But it's nearly summer, dear. You'll roast yourself! How about a nice, spring jacket?"

"No!" said Anna. When her mind was made up, she rarely changed it.

"If I do get you a bright, blue coat with fur lining, then will you behave?" asked her father.

"Maybe," said Anna.

Mrs Marple grabbed her daughter by the ear. "Mr Mango Muldoon, the proprietor of this hotel, has kindly ordered a taxi for us. It is presently waiting outside with its meter running." And with that Mrs Marple gave her daughter's ear a commanding tug.

Chapter Five

THE CROWD AROUND Buckingham Palace was particularly thick that day. People from all different lands were pressed tightly together to catch a glimpse of some of the Queen's horses and some of the Queen's men, if not the actual Queen herself.

Amongst the crowd were three strange-looking men dressed in large Mexican hats with very broad brims, called "sombreros," and colourful blanket-like Mexican shawls, called "serapes." One of the men was very fat and was smoking a cheap cigar. Another was short and wore his sombrero over his eyes. The third had very thick glasses and a bright, red nose. They were, of course, the jewel thieves disguised in Mexican clothing. No one saw as they quickly ducked into the shrubbery which surrounded the Queen's Palace.

At the same time as the jewel thieves were searching for the lost bag of diamonds which had been left in the shrubs when the gang had made their escape, a black taxi pulled up in front of the Palace and out walked a very tired Marple family. In the last half hour they had rushed through every inch of the Tate gallery but they had only been able to take a quick dash around the British Museum in order to keep on schedule.

They were met by one of the Queen's Guards, a tall young man wearing a furry black hat (which actually looked like a muffler stood on its end), a bright, scarlet tunic, and high black boots that were polished so bright you could have seen the reflection of the sun, had there been any sun to reflect.

"May I help you?" said the Queen's guard, holding his rifle in such a way as to bring them to a stop.

"Yes," said Mrs Marple. "We have an appointment to meet the Queen. I believe she's expecting us for tea. You can tell her the Marple family is here."

"I'm terribly sorry," said the Queen's guard, "but Her Majesty isn't having any visitors today..."

"That's ridiculous," said Mr Marple. "We've come all the way from Prairieview, Iowa to see her!"

"Quite unfortunate," said the Queen's Guard, "because something happened early this morning that upset Her Majesty, so she has had to cancel all her appointments. You see, a bag of her precious jewels were stolen."

"How terrible!" said Mrs Marple. "You will give her our condolences, won't you? And tell her that if there's anything we can do for her, just call."

"Certainly," said the guard. And with that, he stiffened his body like a toy soldier and came abruptly to attention.

"Well," said Mr Marple, as they walked away, "I guess that's that. It would have been nice to have asked her about ordering some of our tea cosies..."

But Mrs Marple wasn't as forgiving as her husband. "I think she should have swallowed her pride and seen us no matter what. After all, if the situations were reversed and she had travelled all the way from London to Prairieview, Iowa to visit us, we wouldn't have stood her up even if our jewels had been stolen," she said somewhat grumpily.

"We don't have any jewels," Mr Marple reminded her.

Anna, however, didn't regret it in the least. "I'm glad she didn't invite us in," she said. "I didn't want to see her anyway. She might have cut off my head if I had spilled as much as a drop of milk on her precious carpet when I poured it in my cup!"

"Nonsense," said Mrs Marple. "She has servants who pour the milk. She wouldn't let a guest pour it for herself!"

"That's awful!" Anna replied. "People should be allowed to pour their own milk! I bet she gets to pour her own milk, doesn't she!"

"What would be the point of being Queen if you went ahead and poured your own milk, Anna?" Mrs Marple said in exasperation.

While Mrs Marple and her daughter were debating the proper etiquette for pouring milk at royal teas, Mr Marple suddenly had an urgent call from nature. It sounded something like this:

"Hello, Mr Marple. This is nature calling. You had a bit too much coffee this morning and you were rushing around so much that you didn't stop at you-know-where to do you-know-what when I told you to. Well, now you're not going a single step further until you do you-know-what wherever!"

And at that very moment, Mr Marple stopped dead in his tracks and crossed his legs (which is a very difficult thing to do when you are standing upright). He looked quite uncomfortable.

"Whatever's the matter with you?" asked Mrs Marple. Mr Marple's face turned red and he whispered something into Mrs Marple's ear.

"I guess you could ask them to let you inside the palace to use the bathroom if you promise to hurry," said Mrs Marple.

But Mr Marple had his pride. "No," he said, "not in there. Do you suppose it would be rude if I did it in the bushes?" he asked in a very hushed voice.

"Well, if you do it very fast. I'll stand in front so no one can see," Mrs Marple offered, understanding, as someone with a very weak bladder herself, the urgency of the situation.

"I wouldn't go in there if I were you," said Anna, who being a bright child knew exactly what was happening, though she couldn't understand why her parents were being so coy about a simple matter of going to the toilet.

"For Heaven's sake, Anna," scolded her mother, "do keep still!"

"Well, don't say I didn't warn you if you get jumped on by a gang of Mexican bandits!" Anna said with a shrug. She had seen three sombreros bouncing about in the shrubbery and had thought that a bit suspicious.

But Mr Marple was in too much of a hurry to listen and he quickly disappeared into the bushes which surrounded the palace. However, moments later, as he was zipping up his trousers, he noticed a velvet bag on the ground hidden in the bramble. And as he was a naturally curious person, he bent down to pick it up, thinking, of course, that he was unnoticed.

A few feet away, Fat Al, Little Albert and Henry-the-Nose, who were on all fours, quietly searching every inch of the ground for the lost bag of diamonds, watched in horror as Mr Marple picked up the velvet bag and undid the ribbon. Then, as he took out one of the precious gems and held it up to the shadowy light that had managed to penetrate through the gorsey shrubs, they saw his face suddenly change from mild curiosity to paralytic shock. And they even saw his guilty eyes when, after a moment of thought, he looked to his right and then to his left before stealthily placing the little velvet bag into his jacket pocket.

"Oi!" whispered Henry-the-Nose into Fat Al's ear. "'at bloke's nicked our loot!"

"Do you think we should jump him?" asked Little Albert in a hushed voice.

"Right!" whispered Fat Al. "On the count of three..."

But before Fat Al could even start to count, Mrs Marple shouted, "Hurry up! Someone's coming!" And hearing his wife holler, Mr Marple jumped out of the shrubs and, smiling nervously said, "My, that feels good! Now let's get out of here!"

"Why such a hurry?" said Mrs Marple as she was being dragged along by her husband. "We have an excess of fifteen minutes since the Queen cancelled out on us. So you needn't pull so hard."

"Our driver is waiting to take us around London, remember? And his meter is still running," Mr Marple replied, quickening his pace.

"Yes, that's true," said Mrs Marple. "Time is money."

And looking behind her, she shouted, "Anna, hurry up, won't you?"

Back in the bushes, the gang watched in horror as Mr Marple and their loot was quickly disappearing from view.

"What do we do now?" asked Little Albert.

Fat Al bit down on his smelly cigar. "We'll follow 'em lads! And we won't let 'em out of our sight wherever they go or whatever they do until we get the loot back that's rightfully ours!"

Chapter Six

WHEN THE MARPLE family piled back inside their waiting taxi, the driver, who had been spending his time trying to figure out how he should invest the money from what was certain to be a stupendous fare, said, "Where to, guv?"

"Anywhere," said Mr Marple, sounding strangely like a minor character in a gangster film, "only step on it and fast!"

"But we're not due at the Tower of London till three forty-five," said Mrs Marpel. And then, checking her watch, she said, "That leaves one hour and thirty-seven minutes with nothing planned." Suddenly she felt a chill come over her. "Oh, my Lord!" she cried, clutching her husband's clammy hand. "What will we do?"

"Don't panic!" shouted Mr Marple, in a panicky sort of way. And then catching hold of himself again, he said, "Surely we'll think of something." But he could as easily have been speaking to himself as to his wife.

For he could feel the precious jewels burning in his pocket.

Tomorrow they were leaving for France. And that meant he had to decide what to do with the diamonds now. He knew that when they crossed the border they would have to go through customs. And you never knew if your pockets would be checked by the customs men who would surely want to know if you were bringing stolen diamonds into their country. (Which is why it always pays to have a clean hanky in your trousers when travelling abroad.)

"Maybe you and the lady would like to do a little shopping, guv," suggested the driver, who had bravely taken many American tourists on shopping safaris through the wilds of London.

Suddenly something clicked inside Mr Marple's head. "That's right," he shouted. And turning to his daughter, he said, "Didn't we promise you a new coat?"

"Yes," said Anna, pleased that he had remembered. "Blue with fur lining," she reminded him.

"Do you know where we might buy a coat such as that?" Mr Marple asked the driver.

"I know a shop that's certain to have a coat like that, guv!" said the driver. And he drove off in the direction of a place called Soho.

The Soho establishment of Mr Mark and Mr Spencer Farouk, so highly recommended by the taxi driver, had, unfortunately suffered a sudden flood from a burst water main and, the staff (namely Mr Mark and Mr Spencer Farouk, themselves) had been temporarily forced to sell their wares from a pushcart in a deserted alley. But when Anna described the specifications of the coat she wanted, Mr Spencer Farouk snapped his fingers and said, "No problem!"

Then whispering some instructions to his cousin, Mr Mark, he invited the Marples to look at his other fine items such as 15th century snuff boxes, original reproductions of the Mona Lisa, and a wide array of naughty night-gowns.

Very shortly, however, Mr Mark returned with a box. And opening it, Anna found a beautiful, blue coat with fur lining. It was exactly what she had wanted.

"Try it on first, dear, before you decide," her mother wisely suggested.

Anna did just that. And except for the minor question of the blue dye which hadn't completely dried, the coat was perfect. Anna even liked the idea of the jagged trim around the bottom, as it gave the garment a primitive look which was so much the fashion. And if the fur was actually nylon wigs which had been cut into strips and then tacked to the interior of the coat, the feel was luxuriant. And that's what mattered most to her.

Mr Marple, too, was pleased. Especially when he heard that the price was only ninety-nine pounds and ninety-nine pence (as a garment of similar quality would have cost at least twice that much in Prairieview, Iowa).

"Are you sure you like it?" he asked his daughter. "I mean if I pay all that money I want to know that you'll wear it – at least for a while."

"It's beautiful!" Anna enthused. "It's something I've always wanted!"

"But isn't it a little warm for summer, dear?" asked Mrs Marple.

"I love being hot!" said Anna. "I'll wear it even if the temperature is 100!"

So Mr Marple paid for the purchase with his credit card, gratefully accepted by Mr Spencer Farouk, who rang up the sale after a quick trip to the neighbouring telephone kiosk.

Then Mr and Mrs Marple and Anna piled back into the taxi and drove off, unaware that their movements were being closely watched by the gang of jewel thieves, who had followed them on their push bike, still dressed in their Mexican disguises.

Chapter Seven

THE NEXT MORNING Mr and Mrs Marple awoke bright and early, anxious for the new day to begin. Anna, who was still in bed, had slept in her new coat, as Mr Marple had known she would, since it was her habit to sleep in anything new so that she had a chance to break it in properly. However, what Anna didn't know, since she was such a sound sleeper, was that in the middle of the night her father had crept over to her bedside and had sewn the bag of diamonds into the lining. Then, satisfied that the jewels would never be discovered by prying customs agents, he went back to bed and slept quite well considering how loudly Mrs Marple snored.

So Mr Marple was quite chipper when he bounded out of bed that morning. "I wonder what's for breakfast?" he asked, as he did his stretching exercises which he hoped would do something for his figure but never really seemed to make any difference whatsoever.

"Prepare yourself for a treat!" said Mrs Marple. "In

the full colour brochure which the travel agent gave us, it says, "'Mr Mango Muldoon prides himself on serving his guests the Great English Breakfast of curried corn flakes, boiled cucumber and gingered yoghurt.'"

"I'm glad we're staying someplace that serves traditional food. When you travel, it's important to be able to experience the true culture," Mr Marple replied. Then, taking his wife's hand and giving it a pat, he said, "You know, dear, I'm so glad you talked me into taking this trip."

"Yes. It was the right thing to do, I suppose. But to tell the truth, I'm just a little worried how we'll pay for it when we get home," Mrs Marple replied, looking into his eyes and displaying a touch of remorse.

"Don't concern yourself about that," said Mr Marple, reassuringly. "Somehow I think it will all work itself out."

"I suppose you're right," said Mrs Marple. Though she couldn't help but wonder about her husband's newfound optimism.

However, unknown to the Marples, as they were preparing themselves for breakfast, something strange was taking place in the kitchen. In fact, it was quite peculiar. For instead of preparing the Great English Breakfast of curried corn flakes, boiled cucumber and gingered yoghurt for his guests, Mr Mango Muldoon was sitting quietly in the broom closet. Although, if the truth be known, he didn't particularly want to be there. In fact, if he hadn't been bound and gagged and tied to a chair, he certainly wouldn't have remained in the broom closet at the very time his guests expected him to be seeing to their gastronomic needs. Yet there he was at half past seven staring at the mops and sponges and polyethylene buckets while three unfamiliar faces were gathering around the kitchen table. Of course, you don't have to be a great detective to guess who they were. But, then again, even great detectives are wrong sometimes.

In this case, however, the great detective would have been right. For gathered around the kitchen table was our gang of desperate jewel thieves who had come very, very early and had tied poor Mr Mango Muldoon with his own laundry line, gagging him with the morning newspaper they had found outside the door. Then they had put him in the broom closet – not out of nastiness, but because they didn't want anyone who happened along asking why Mr Mango Muldoon was tied up in his chair.

Now they sat around the table in Mr Mango Muldoon's kitchen and discussed what they would do next.

"Who has a plan?" asked Fat Al.

"I thought you did," said Little Albert.

"I do," said Fat Al. "I just wondered whether there were any others."

Henry-the-Nose raised his hand. "I got a plan, Fat Al!" he said.

"I was afraid of that," said Fat Al. "All right, what's your plan?"

"My plan is to get back our loot!" said Henry-the-Nose. And then he looked from Fat Al to Little Albert to see if either of them appreciated the brilliant simplicity of his logic.

"That's not a plan," said Fat Al. "That's what we want to accomplish."

"What d'yer mean it's not a plan?" asked Henry-the-

Nose. "Wouldn't you say, 'I plan to eat a sausage,' if you wanted to eat one, but didn't 'ave it yet?"

"That's a different kind of plan, banana nose!" said Fat Al. "The plan we mean is the kind that tells you how to get the sausage that you want to eat!"

"Well, I got 'at sort of plan, too!" said Henry-the-Nose. "Me plan is to grab it and skedaddle!"

Fat Al closed his eyes and counted to ten while Little Albert tried explaining to Henry-the-Nose that they were agreed on taking back the diamonds. The question was how to find them.

While this discussion was getting more and more confusing, the dining room was beginning to fill up with guests, among whom were the Marples.

"I wonder where our food is?" asked Mrs Marple. "I'm very, very hungry and we've been waiting for almost three and a half minutes."

"That's not right, keeping a hungry person waiting so long," Mr Marple agreed. "In Prairieview we would have eaten and been halfway home by now."

"Perhaps someone should make sure that Mr Muldoon isn't tied up in the broom closet," said Anna.

"Well, don't you have a wild imagination!" said Mrs Marple. "But perhaps I'll just stick my head in the door of the kitchen, just to give a look-see."

And with that, Mrs Marple went over to the kitchen door and peeked her head through. "Yoohoo," she called out. "Mr Muldoon, we're all in the dining room waiting for our Great English Breakfasts!"

"Coming up!" said Fat Al, as he blew some smoke from his cheap cigar at the face peeking through the crack in the door.

When the door had closed again, Little Albert looked at Fat Al and said, "What are we going to give 'em? I can't cook! Can you?"

Fat Al looked at Henry-the-Nose. "He'll make 'em a Great English Breakfast while we search their room."

Henry-the-Nose opened his google-eyes wide as saucers. "Why me?"

"Because you're the only one who knows how to cook," said Fat Al.

"But what's a Great English Breakfast?" asked Henry-the-Nose.

"Fried kippers and beans," said Little Albert.

"Naw," said Fat Al. "It's sausage and mash."

"I thought it was porridge and curds," said Henry-the-Nose.

"Just see what there is in the fridge," said Fat Al, "and grill it."

Henry-the-Nose watched his friends sneak out the back door to the rear stairs and said, "I never 'ave any fun!"

So, as the Marples tasted the delights of the Great English Breakfast which Henry-the-Nose had prepared for them (namely grilled brussels sprouts on crumpets in a delectable sauce of milky tea) they were unaware that their luggage was being meticulously searched by Little Albert while Fat Al checked every nook and cranny of their room (including prying loose some squeaky floor boards) in an effort to find the missing loot.

What the gang couldn't have guessed, however, was that the stolen jewels weren't in the room at all. For, as we know, they had been sewn into the lining of Anna's coat late last night and, since Anna wouldn't take her coat off, the jewels were presently going every place she went.

Presently they were with her as she was eating her Great English Breakfast of grilled brussels sprouts on crumpets with milky tea sauce while she wondered whether curried corn flakes would have tasted any worse.

"You know, Anna, you really should take your coat off while you're eating," said her mother. "People will think you're anxious to leave."

"I am anxious to leave," said Anna. "Can't we go someplace for a hamburger?"

"No," said Mrs Marple. "We've gone five thousand miles so that you can experience other types of cuisine and you ask for a hamburger! I mean, really, young lady, it's quite inexcusable! Take off your coat this instant and eat your Great English Breakfast!"

"Let her wear her coat if she wants," said Mr Marple to his wife. "After all, if she's wearing it, she's certain not to lose it – unless, of course, she loses herself."

Mrs Marple frowned at her husband's contradictory remarks, but as it was nearly time to go, she decided to give in. "Then hurry up and finish," she said, reluctantly. "Our taxi will be here very shortly to take us to the airport."

So, holding her nose, Anna gobbled down the last of the grilled sprouts while her father went off to settle the bill.

Mr Marple, of course, couldn't find Mr Mango Muldoon anywhere, for, as we know, Mr Muldoon had been tied up by the gang and was presently in the broom closet, unable to attend to his duties. Therefore, Mr Marple went into the kitchen to ask the chef (who we also know was none other than Henry-the-Nose) whether he knew where the proprietor was so he could settle his account.

Henry-the-Nose was so startled at seeing Mr Marple come into the kitchen that he bumped his nose against the hot grill which set off a horrific chain of sneezes of such force and intensity that Henry-the-Nose was thrown back against the crockery shelf, hitting it so hard that all the cups, saucers and dinner plates flew off and crashed to the floor, making an absolutely terrifying racket.

"I hope I haven't disturbed you," said Mr Marple, "but I was wondering if you knew where Mr Mango

Muldoon was right now. I wish to settle my account before leaving."

"Leaving?" said Henry-the-Nose, dusting off bits of broken china from his head and picking himself up from the floor. "Oi! You can't leave yet!"

"I'm sorry," said Mr Marple. "I know it was a very short stay, but we're due in Paris this very day."

"Paris!" shouted Henry-the-Nose. "'at's in France! I'n'it?"

"Yes," said Mr Marple. "That's why we're going there. My wife insists on seeing at least three countries during our five day holiday – England, France and Italy. Fortunately, the Spanish Steps are not in Spain, for if they were she would have insisted on going to four countries and that would have been too much, don't you think?"

Henry-the-Nose didn't know what to think. But he decided that if he ever was to try thinking, now was the time. So he closed his eyes and took a great, big breath and thought. And suddenly an idea came to him. And this was the clever thing he said: "Listen, mate. Mr Muldoon is all tied up. Too bad, i'n'it? Oi! I got an idea! You give me the address where you'll be in Paris and I'll 'ave 'im send you the bill. 'ow's 'at?"

"A very good idea, young man," said Mr Marple. "We'll be staying at the Hotel de Paris, a small but charming place (it says in the brochure) on the Rue Bonaparte, run by a gentleman by the name of Mohammed De Gaul. Mr Muldoon can send the bill there." And, with that, Mr Marple went upstairs to his room where he found his wife and daughter commenting on the terrible housekeeping of this otherwise lovely hotel.

"Just look at this mess!" said Mrs Marple. "You would think they'd learn to make the bed a little better than that!"

"Well," said Mr Marple, grabbing one of the suitcases, "We're leaving anyway. Our taxi will be waiting for us by now." And he took his daughter by the hand, while Mrs Marple took the other suitcase and, together, they trooped out the door.

Peeking from under the bed, Fat Al and Little Albert watched them go.

Chapter Eight

WHEN THEIR PLANE had landed at the Paris airport, Mrs Marple thought her husband looked rather upset. In fact, he was. For, although Mr Marple was quite sure that the customs inspectors would never search his daughter's new coat – especially since his daughter was still inside – it was his first attempt at smuggling stolen jewels into a foreign country and he didn't know quite what to expect. So, in order to keep his spirits up, he thought of all the wonderful things he could do once the diamonds were sold. Perhaps he would expand his tea cosy business and even go into a new line – he had been thinking of sweaters for coffee pots or, perhaps, jogging suits for milk pitchers. Certainly, with the proceeds – tax free, of course – from these precious gems anything would be possible. And, as he thought of this, he rubbed his hands with glee.

But when, at last, it was his turn to answer the simple question asked by the very bored official whose job it was to ask over and over and over again

– "Do you have anyzing to declare?" – Mr Marple's nerve suddenly gave way and he replied, "Nooooo. I have nothing to declare. Nothing at all. Not even the diamonds that were stolen from the Queen the other day. Hahahahaha. Imagine me trying to bring stolen diamonds into France? Ridiculous, isn't it?"

Because of that, Mrs Marple and Anna had to wait hours while Mr Marple was searched in the adjoining room by a team of special customs agents and three bloodhounds who were trained to sniff out diamonds, rubies and forged ten franc notes. When it was all over, Mr Marple was severely cautioned not to make jokes about smuggling stolen jewels. But, for his trouble, he was given a complementary ticket for a half-bottle of champagne at the Folies-Bergère.

So the family, once more united, and slightly shaken by their rude welcoming, hailed a taxi and headed straight for their hotel. Little did they know that right behind them were Fat Al, Little Albert and Henry-the-Nose, dressed up as French Apache dancers, with black berets and black trousers and black and white striped shirts and thin little moustaches painted on their upper lips.

"Follow zat cab!" ordered Fat Al as the gang piled into a taxi.

"But zere are so many cabs," said the driver. "And zey are all going to zee same place – Paree."

"Zen take us to ze hotel of Monsieur Mohammed De Gaul on Rue Bonaparte," Fat Al commanded.

"At your zervice," said the driver. And off he went.

"You speak French very well," complimented Little Albert.

"Yes," said Fat Al, "that's because I used to listen to Maurice Chevalier sing 'Every Little Breeze Seems to Whisper Louise' on the radio when I was a lad."

"I wonder what 'Louise' means in French?" asked Little Albert.

"Maybe it means 'snail,' said Henry-the-Nose. "When a breeze whispers something to me, it usually means I'm 'ungry and I need to eat. The French love to eat snails, don't 'ey?"

"Don't be daft!" said Little Albert. "Nobody would eat anything as slimy as a snail! That's absolutely disgusting!"

"The French eat lots of disgusting things," said Fat Al.

"They eat the hind legs of frogs..."

"Oi!" said Henry-the-Nose, quite outraged. "Do you mean 'ey eat the legs of poor, defenceless little froggies?"

"They do," insisted Fat Al. "And they eat the stomach of cows!"

"Let's go back home right now!" said Little Albert. "I don't care about the diamonds if we have to eat food like that!"

"Don't worry," said Fat Al opening up his bag. "You don't think I'd leave England without taking proper precautions!" And he puled out two large cans of baked beans, a box of frozen fish fingers (now thawed) and a bottle of orange squash.

Meanwhile, unaware that they were being followed by the gang of jewel thieves, Mrs Marple was reading the day's itinerary to her husband and daughter while the taxi raced on toward the centre of Paris.

"First, we will check into our hotel, take a shower (being careful, of course, not to drink the water) and change our clothes. That should take thirteen and a half minutes. Then we will grab a quick bite to eat at Maxim's, where I understand you can get the world's most delicious hot dogs – ten minutes and twenty-five seconds. Then we can spend twenty full minutes at the Louvre. After that, we'll run down to the river and take a quick tour of the Seine – three minutes and eighteen seconds – and then, since we'll be right by the Champs Elysees, we'll walk very fast up to the Arc de Triomphe and then run back again, which should take about six minutes in all, but, they say, if you go to Paris you should spend some time strolling down the Champs Elysées..."

"When do we get to go to the Eiffel Tower?" asked Anna.

"The Eiffel Tower?" replied Mrs Marple. "Let's see..." And she scoured her schedule but failed to find any mention of the Eiffel Tower. "My goodness," she said, "I've forgotten to schedule it in."

"Well, then schedule it," said Mr Marple.

"But how?" asked Mrs Marple, showing him the page. "Every single minute is accounted for!"

"Can't you cancel something and replace it with a

visit to the Eiffel Tower?"

"No. It's not that easy. It would throw the timing off! And you, as a factory owner, know how important it is to time things very precisely," said Mrs Marple.

"But I want to see the Eiffel Tower! That's all I want to see and we've come all the way to Paris and I want to see it!" Anna whined.

"There must be something we could change," said Mr Marple to his wife. "After all, we have come all this way and it would be a shame if we didn't see the Eiffel Tower."

"Then there's only one thing to do," said Mrs Marple. "You and Anna can stay in the taxi and continue on to the Eiffel Tower. I will go to the hotel and check in. Then, in twenty minutes, you can meet me at the Louvre."

"Agreed," said Mr Marple. And, as he spoke, the taxi pulled up in front of the hotel. Mr Marple helped his wife inside with the luggage. Then he got back into the cab and he and Anna went off again, toward the Eiffel Tower.

Chapter Nine

MOMENTS LATER, THE taxi carrying Fat Al, Little Albert and Henry-the-Nose pulled up in front of the hotel. "Voila!" said the driver, "Zis is ze 'otel you 'ave asked for. Is it not?" Fat Al looked up at the sign. It read: "Hotel de Paris. Mohammed De Gaul, Prop."

"Yes," he said to the driver. "Zis must be zee place." And the three French Apache dancers piled out of the cab and walked up to the door of the hotel.

Unfortunately, they all tried to go inside at once. But it was quite obvious that the door was too narrow for the three of them to fit through all together. So Fat Al stepped back a pace, and bowed (sarcastically), tipped his beret, made a face and said, "After you."

Then Henry-the-Nose and Little Albert both tried to go through the door at the same time. Of course they collided, and, of course, Henry bumped his nose which made him sneeze profusely. And while Henry was sneezing and Little Albert was wiping himself off, Fat Al decided to walk through the door. But just as he was going through, someone was trying to come out at the same time. And the person coming out, an elderly lady from New York who was carrying a little Pekinese dog, bumped into Fat Al's very large tummy and bounced back inside, dropping her doggy and the bundle of buttered croissants she was taking with her to the park. To the lady's dismay, the doggy immediately started eating the croissants. Fat Al, now inside, tried to help her pick them up. But just as he bent over, Little Albert came bounding through the door and knocked Fat Al onto his bottom. And then, as Little Albert tried to help Fat Al up, Henry-the-Nose came in, bumping Little Albert who fell on top of Fat Al. And they both lay in a heap on the floor.

Henry-the-Nose, who had been sneezing so much he no longer knew what was going on, then said, "Why is everybody sitting on the floor? 'at's not very polite even in France, I'll wager!"

That comment angered Fat Al so much that he got up and tweaked Henry's nose very, very hard. This set off another series of sneezes that terrified the Pekinese who dropped the last croissant it had been eating and dashed, frantically, out of the open door. The lady from New York ran after it screaming, "Fifi, darling! Come back to Mommy!"

"Now see what you've done!" said Fat Al accusingly.

"Me?" asked Henry-the-Nose, pointing to himself. "What did I do?"

By this time, the proprietor of the hotel, Mohammed De Gaul, had come over to see what all the fuss was about.

"May I 'elp you, monsieurs?" he asked, twirling his long, waxy moustache and looking at them severely through a pair of pince-nez glasses.

The three Apache dancers looked at one another.

"Maybe you can," said Fat Al. And then he said to the proprietor, "We are looking for someone..."

"Someone?" said the proprietor, twirling his moustache again and considering the question. "Ah, yes. Now let me think. I know I 'ave 'eard zat name before..." And he thought and he thought. And as he thought, he continued to twirl his moustache until it snapped off right there in his hand, causing him much distress and embarrassment. And he rushed, immediately, into his office to find his moustache repair kit.

"Quick!" said Fat Al. "While he's away, we'll check the guest register!"

The three Apache dancers rushed over to the desk and grabbed the guest register and flipped through the pages until they found the notation they were looking for: "M. Marple and family – Room 419."

Then they all rushed into the lift together.

"Can I push the button?" asked Henry-the-Nose and Little Albert simultaneously.

"Who pushed it last time?" asked Fat Al.

"He did!" both Little Albert and Henry-the-Nose said, pointing at each other.

Fat Al closed his eyes. "You're both a bunch of twits!" he said, pushing the button himself, which made Henry-the-Nose and Little Albert feel like sulking. So, as the elevator was lifted to the fourth floor, Little Albert crouched in one corner and Henry-the-Nose crouched in the other and both of them made faces at each other.

When they got to the fourth floor, Fat Al gave them a pep talk because they were both being so moody.

"Listen, lads," he said, "we've come all this way to get back our loot and we don't want to spoil it now!"

"He's right," said Little Albert, looking at Henry-the-Nose. "Do you want to shake hands?"

So Little Albert and Henry-the-Nose shook hands. And then Little Albert and Fat Al shook hands. And then Fat Al and Henry-the-Nose shook hands. And then Fat Al, Henry-the-Nose and Little Albert all shook hands together.

"Oi! Let's do it again!" said Henry-the-Nose, who couldn't remember the last time he had such a good time.

But before anyone had time to answer, the door to Room 419 opened and out walked Mrs Marple.

"Oh," she said, seeing the three men dressed up in costume, "are you honest-to-goodness French Apache dancers? I've always wanted to met Apache dancers! My name is Mrs Marple and I'm from Prairieview, Iowa..."

Suddenly, Fat Al had a brilliant idea. "Oui, Madame," he said in his best French, "we are ze famous Apache dancers of Paree and we have come to dance with you!"

Mrs Marple was delighted. "Imagine that!" she said. "How thoughtful of the French Tourist Board to send a troupe of Apache dancers to the hotels to entertain the guests!" And then, glancing down at her watch, she said, "I have just time enough for a thirty-five second Apache dance before I leave for the Louvre."

"Thirty-five seconds is more zan enough!" said Fat Al as he grabbed Mrs Marple in his arms and danced her back into her room, twirling and dipping like a real Apache dancer, until he had danced her over to a chair. Whereupon, Little Albert and Henry-the-Nose threw a rope around her and danced in a circle till she was all tied up!

"Is this part of the dance?" she asked.

"Oui, Madame," said Fat Al. "Zis is ze traditional Apache dance. And you have done it very well. It is too bad your husband isn't here to see, because you are one of the best American tourist Apache dancers zat I have ever danced with."

"I'm so pleased!" said Mrs Marple, blushing slightly.

"And it's such a shame that Mr Marple wasn't here. He would have enjoyed your performance greatly. But, alas, he is presently at the Eiffel Tower with our daughter, Anna."

"Ze Eifeel Tower?" asked Fat Al, lifting his eyebrows.

"No, THE EIFFEL TOWER," said Mrs Marple a little louder, thinking the Apache dancers might have a bit of trouble understanding English.

And hearing this, the three Apache dancers raced from the room, leaving poor Mrs Marple all tied up in knots and shouting, "Is it over? Yoohoo! Mr Apache dancers! I've only ten seconds left..."

Unfortunately, no one could hear her as the gang had slammed the door behind them.

Fat Al, Henry-the-Nose and Little Albert dashed back to the elevator and all together pressed the button for going down. Then, when the door opened, they raced through the lobby and then, one at a time, through the front door, and bounded into a waiting taxi.

"Ze Eifeel Tower!" shouted Fat Al to the driver. "Do you know where zat is?"

"Oui, oui," said the driver.

"Zen 'urry!" said Fat Al. "And if you get zere very, very fast, I'll make eet worth you while!"

And saying "Oui, oui," once again, the driver headed off, lickity split.

"How will you make it worth his while?" whispered Little Albert into Fat Al's ear as they sped down the road.

"I'll give him one of our frozen fish fingers," Fat Al whispered back. "They've become a little soggy anyway."

"I like 'em soggy," said Henry-the-Nose, who had overheard.

"Don't worry," said Fat Al. "There's plenty more where those came from once we get our loot back!"

Chapter Ten

AS THE GANG was speeding toward the Eiffel Tower, Mr Marple and Anna were on the second level, enjoying the view. They had walked all the way up because Anna had insisted, and now, after a few minutes of recuperative wheezes, Mr Marple was showing her the sights.

"It's too bad we're always racing around so fast," said Anna, "because I would have liked a closer look at all those little toy houses and people."

"Ha, ha, ha!" laughed Mr Marple. "They only look little because we're so very far up and they're so very far down."

"I meant the toy collection at the exhibit over by the fountain that we passed," she said, pointing in the direction of the symmetrical garden below.

"Well," said Mr Marple, "maybe we'll have a few seconds to look at it on our way back. But, for now, I think we deserve a little drink, don't you? After all, it's very hot and we did climb a long way and you're wearing a fur-lined coat..."

So Mr Marple and Anna walked over to the little café which was serving the typical French summertime drink of Coca Cola in plastic cups.

Meanwhile the gang had arrived at the bottom of the Eiffel Tower and had bounded out of their taxi after having paid the fare and having left a frozen fish finger as a tip (which the driver stared at for several seconds before tossing out the window – whereupon a gendarme came up to him and shouted that he should have put his litter into a proper rubbish bin and then a tremendous argument ensued bringing in many bystanders two of whom fell in love and eventually were married, but that's another story).

When the gang had got to the second level and had spotted Mr Marple and Anna at the little outdoor café, Fat Al whispered something to Little Albert and Henry-the-Nose. Then they went up to where Mr Marple and Anna were sitting.

"Are you Monsieur Marple?" asked Fat Al.

Mr Marple looked up somewhat surprised to see a French Apache dancer with a very large tummy who knew his name. "Yes," he said. "I'm Mr Marple. Who are you?"

"I'm from ze French Police. We 'ave reason to believe zat you 'ave in your possession ze Queen's jewels zat was nicked by zome ozer lads before!"

Mr Marple tried to make sense out of all those muddled words and, when he did, he suddenly turned blue in the face, because this accusation, coming so unexpectedly like that, had made the Coca Cola he was drinking go down the wrong pipe. And he began to cough, quite excitedly, till his eyes began to spin in little circles.

Henry-the-Nose knew what that felt like because, as we know, he had something of a sneezing problem himself. So he patted Mr Marple on the back and tried to console him. "It would 'elp if yer put yer 'ands up in the air, mate," he said.

Mr Marple put his hands up in the air and soon stopped coughing. But he kept his hands up even afterward because he thought that Henry-the-Nose was really a French policeman who wanted him to put his hands up because he was going to arrest him, not because he wanted to help him stop coughing.

Of course, everyone on the second level of the Eiffel Tower began to stare at them, which was quite embarrassing. So Fat Al said, "Put your hands down!"

Mr Marple obediently put his hands down. Though, by this time, he was quite confused and in such a state of anxiety that he started coughing once more.

Henry-the-Nose let out a sympathetic sigh. "Yer better put yer 'ands up again."

"No!" shouted Fat Al. "Keep your hands down!"

"Make up your mind!" said Mr Marple between coughs.

As Henry-the-Nose puzzled over that expression, which his mother would occasionally say to him, and which he never understood because it sounded so much like "Make up your bed," Mr Marple was quickly trying to work out his escape plans.

"If only I had a parachute," Mr Marple said to himself, "I could jump over the side of the Eiffel Tower. Then, once I landed on the ground, I could run very fast to a fancy dress shop and buy a tuxedo. Then I'd take a taxi to the airport and use my credit card to get a ticket to Buenos Aires. I could work there for three or four years picking coffee beans and then, when I'd made my fortune, I'd send for my wife and daughter..."

His dream of escape, however, was interrupted by his daughter who said, "If we're going to sit here for long could I have some money for another Coca Cola?"

Reaching into his pocket, Mr Marple fished out some coins and handed them, silently, to his child.

When Anna went inside the café to buy her drink, Little Albert said, "Mr Marple, I, too, am from the London police. Follow us!"

"But that gentleman said he was from the French police!" exclaimed Mr Marple.

"Oi!" said Henry-the-Nose. "I t'ought you were from the French Police and we were from Scotland Yard!"

"Can't you two do anything right?" Fat Al asked Henry-the-Nose and Little Albert, in a voice that was curdled in exasperation, like sour milk in a cup of chocolate-flavoured tea.

"Really, they were doing the best they could under the circumstances," said Mr Marple, hoping to get a lighter sentence by being co-operative.

"You keep out of this!" said Fat Al.

"Does that mean I can go?" asked Mr Marple.

"No!" said Fat Al, "It means you better follow me or I'll take out my gat and blow your head off!"

"W'at's a 'gat'?" whispered Henry-the-Nose to Little Albert.

Little Albert shrugged. "Maybe it's French for 'bat'"

"Or 'rat'?" Henry-the-Nose suggested.

"You can't blow someone's head off with a rat!" said Little Albert.

"You can if it's a fat rat," Henry-the-Nose responded.

Mr Marple, who didn't want his head blown off either by a 'gat' or a 'fat rat', said, "But what about my daughter, Anna, who's inside the café purchasing a Coca Cola in a plastic cup?"

"Henry-the-Nose will stay with her," said Fat Al. And pointing a menacing finger at Mr Marple, he said, "You come with Little Albert and me! And keep your mouth shut!"

So, not being one to disobey authority, Mr Marple went off, walking sullenly between Fat Al and Little

Albert, not daring to ask where they were taking him and wishing for all the world that he had never heard that fatal call from nature which had got him into all this trouble.

Where Fat Al and Little Albert took Mr Marple was up many more flights of stairs and through a door that was closed to visitors. They climbed and they climbed and finally they got to the platform which was right below the needle at the very top of the Eiffel Tower. And there they tied poor Mr Marple to the metal rail that was built to stop people from falling off the edge. Then they proceeded to do something to him that was awful and terrifying. For there, high above Paris, atop the Eiffel Tower, with the winds whipping and lashing around them, Fat Al and Little Albert took off Mr Marple's shoes and mercilessly began to tickle his feet. They tickled and tickled and tickled until, laughing hysterically, he finally told them what they wanted to know. And when they found out, they dashed down the stairs, back to the second level, leaving Mr Marple just as they had left his wife – tied up in knots.

Chapter Eleven

AT THE CAFÉ on the second level of the Eiffel Tower, Anna and Henry-the-Nose were getting along famously.

"What's your name?" asked Anna, sipping at her drink.

"'enry," said Henry-the-Nose. "What's yours?"

"My name's Anna. Are you a real policeman?"

"No," said Henry-the-Nose. "I was pretending."

"I thought so," said Anna. "You don't look like a real policeman."

"'at's good," said Henry-the-Nose. For the last thing in the world he wanted to look like was a real policeman.

"Do you like mushrooms?" Anna asked, casually, though it was somewhat off the subject.

"Only in me tea," said Henry-the-Nose.

"That's awful!" said Anna, making a face.

"Not as bad as snails," said Henry-the-Nose. "Did you know that the French eat snails?"

"Are snails as bad as grilled brussels sprouts?" asked Anna.

"What's wrong with grilled brussels sprouts?" Henry-the-Nose replied.

"Ugh!" said Anna. "Have you ever tasted them?"

"Tasted 'em? Why I 'ave 'em every morning for breakfast!" said Henry-the-Nose.

"You do?" said Anna in wonder. "Then you must be the bravest, most courageous person in the whole, wide world!"

Henry-the-Nose stared at Anna for a minute as he took in those words. And then he smiled, not a silly smile, but a broad smile of appreciation which went all across his face. For no one, ever, in his whole life had called him brave and courageous before. And it made him feel very, very good.

Just then, Fat Al and Little Albert came back and sat down at the table. Fat Al looked at Little Albert and Little Albert looked at Fat Al. Fat Al motioned secretly toward Anna's coat and Little Albert nodded.

"Hello," said Anna. "Are you two pretending to be policemen, too?"

"Yes," said Little Albert.

"No," said Fat Al. "We're investigating a robbery. We have reason to believe that you're wearing a stolen coat."

"My coat? No, you must be mistaken," said Anna. "My father purchased it with his credit card. I know. I was there."

"So were we," said Little Albert.

"And that's why we know it was stolen," said Fat Al. "The men who sold it to you had lifted it from the Salvation Army used clothing shop."

"Really?" said Anna. And she began to cry. "But I love this coat more than anything else in the world!"

And seeing her cry like that, Henry-the-Nose began to cry, too, because listening to Anna had brought back memories of when he was a child and had lost his favourite toy, a green dragon that he was convinced was a frog even though it had a pointy tail and a jagged row of fins running down it's back.

Then Little Albert began to cry, because the scene was beginning to remind him of a bad film – but he always cried at films, good or bad.

And then Fat Al began to cry, because he wanted to be the leader of a band of jewel thieves, not a babysitter for a little American tourist and two grown-up nincompoops.

As they cried, their tears fell onto Anna's coat, making the dye run so that a little blue puddle started to form under their feet and drifted, like a lazy river, along the floor and then over the edge of the Eiffel Tower where it fell several hundred feet below, eventually dripping onto the cart of an ice cream vendor just as he was about to scoop up a cone of vanilla ice cream for a famous opera singer. The blue dye fell right onto the ice cream cone making the vanilla look like boysenberry and so upset the opera singer, who was allergic to that flavour, he had to cancel the night's performance and lay in bed with the covers over his head till he finally got over the shock.

But Anna, who watched her precious coat turn from a lovely shade of blue to a streaky grey, was horrified. "This isn't my coat!" she shouted. "It's a fake imitation!"

"Then you won't mind if we take it back to London, would you?" asked Fat Al.

"Not at all!" said Anna. "I certainly don't want it now!" And, with that, she took it off and handed it to Fat Al.

"Oi!" shouted Henry-the-Nose (who knew nothing about the diamonds being sewn inside the lining because he was with Anna when the tickle-torture made Mr Marple confess). "You can't take 'er coat! 'at's 'ers! We don't want 'er coat! It wouldn't even fit us! It's the diamonds we're after, not 'er coat!"

"Shut up mush brain!" shouted Fat Al, grabbing the coat.

"Oi! Don't you call me 'mush brain'!" shouted Henry-the-Nose as he grabbed the coat back again.

"She gave it to us, pickle snout!" shouted Little Albert, grabbing the coat from Henry-the-Nose.

"Don't call him 'pickle snout'!" shouted Anna, grabbing the coat from Little Albert. "I think I'll keep it after all, if you're going to be like that!"

"Now see what you've done!" shouted Fat Al trying to grab the coat from Anna. He pulled and tugged but she wouldn't let go.

Then Little Albert started pulling with Fat Al and Henry-the-Nose pulled with Anna. And they tugged this way and that. Sometimes it seemed Anna and Henry-the-Nose would win and sometimes it seemed Fat Al and Little Albert would. But both teams clung on tight and wouldn't let go till Anna, by accident, bumped her elbow into Henry's nose. And Henry-the-Nose, who knew what was going to happen next but didn't want it to happen at that moment, tried to hold it back. But the more he held it back, the more his eyes bulged and his cheeks puffed. And then he couldn't hold it back any more. And he let out the most gigantic sneeze the world has ever known. It was a sneeze so great that it was felt all over Paris. And even though it had been a relatively calm day, everyone's hat was blown off, sending caps and bonnets and derbies and turbans all floating down the River Seine like an armada of tiny ships on their way to an aquarian haberdashery.

But back on the second level of the Eiffel Tower, things were a terrible mess. Tables were turned upside down. Food was scattered over the floor. People were cowering in the corners, fearful that the world had come to an end. And the coat that had caused all this fuss in the first palace – well, here's what happened to it:

When Henry-the-Nose had sneezed, he had naturally let go of his end of the coat, sending Little Albert and Fat Al rolling head over heels, backwards. And the coat – the coat went high into the air, and then over the side of the Eiffel Tower. And picking themselves up, Fat Al and Little Albert and Henry-the-Nose and Anna, still half dazed, leaned over the edge of the platform and watched it drift slowly down toward the ground, like the parachute Mr Marple wished he had when he dreamed of his great escape.

Blue fur coat in flight
NE FOULEZ
PAS LA
PELOUSE

Chapter Twelve

LITTLE ALBERT LOOKED at Fat Al in horror as the coat with the jewels sewn inside floated slowly to the ground. "Blimey!" he shouted, "There goes our loot!" Fat Al chomped down on his smelly cigar. "Well, don't just stand there gawking. Let's go after it!"

So Little Albert and Fat Al took off as fast as they could, down the spiral staircase that led to the bottom of the Eiffel Tower. And behind them came Henry-the-Nose and Anna. Round and round they ran, down the circular stairs, till they felt like spinning tops twirling at a May Day celebration. As they ran, the world seemed to spin with them, and soon it was hard to tell whether they were running on their own or whether they weren't on some wonderful merry-go-round without horses.

"Ooooh!" said Anna as she ran. "I'm getting dizzy! Tee hee!"

"The 'ole world's spinning!" shouted Henry-the-Nose. "Or is it me 'ead? 'ar! 'ar!"

"Faster!" shouted Fat Al.

"I'm running as fast as I can!" shouted Little Albert. "Hehe ... I can't see my feet anymore! I'm flying, I think! Haha!"

"It isn't funny!" shouted Fat Al. "All our loot's getting away!" And then he started to giggle too. "Hoohoo!"

And as they ran, round and round, down and down, their laughter became more and more uncontrollable, like when you roll down a hill and a laugh rolls with you and the faster you roll, the faster the laugh rolls, too. And in their spinning minds, all the laughter seemed to echo, with Anna's "Teehees" and Fat Al's "Hoohoos" and Henry-the-Nose's "ar'ars" and Little Albert's "Hahas" all mixing together into a wonderful chorus of giggles that sounded, in a strange way, like what would happen in a feather factory if a cat and dog got in and started chasing each other.

And all this got faster and faster and louder and louder and funnier and funnier until they finally reached the bottom. But by then they were so used to running in circles and were so dizzy, that they continued to spin, like whirling dervishes, round and round and round, till they all fell down. And even then they continued to laugh and laugh until Fat Al looked up and saw the coat float right by his nose and along the pebbled pathway, till it reached a little grassy area where it plopped down.

"Hoohoo!" laughed Fat Al, trying to point. "There it is!"

"Haha!" laughed Little Albert. "There what is?"

"Hoohoo!" laughed Fat Al. "The coat, mutton head!"

"Teehee! I want my coat back!" laughed Anna.

"'ar! 'ar! It's 'ers!" laughed Henry-the-Nose.

And still laughing, they all crawled over to the grassy area where the coat had drifted. But as they tried to crawl up onto the grass, they found their path blocked by a French gendarme who was looking at them very severely and was shaking his head.

"Oh, blimey!" said Little Albert, feeling trouble afoot.

"Let me handle this," said Fat Al.

"Fat Al speaks French," said Henry-the-Nose to Anna.

Fat Al stood up and addressed the gendarme politely. "We wishez to gettez zee coatez for ze little girlez."

The gendarme shook his head, sternly, and pointed his baton at a sign.

"What does it say, Fat Al?" asked Little Albert.

Even though he spoke the language very well, Fat Al had a bit of a problem reading it. Fortunately, the sign was written in many languages – one of which was English. "The sign says 'It is forbidden to walk on the grass'," said Fat Al.

"What do we do now?" asked Little Albert.

And they all stared at the coat lying peacefully in the centre of the small patch of grass till Fat Al had another one of his brilliant ideas which he whispered into the ear of Little Albert.

Immediately, Little Albert went over to a nearby crepe stand and borrowed the pole which was used to hold up a side of the awning (when the proprietor wasn't looking) and then took out of his pocket some of the extra rope that had been used to tie Mr and Mrs Marple and attached it to the pole, making a primitive fishing line. At the end, he fixed a hook made out of a bent nail he had found on the road the other day and had placed in his jacket pocket because you never know when a bent nail will come in handy. Then he took the whole thing back to the patch of grass and began fishing for the coat.

The gendarme looked quite perplexed when he saw what Little Albert was doing. And taking out a thick book of official rules which he carried under his hat so that he would have it at the ready for times such as these, he began to quickly leaf through the well-worn pages, desperately looking for a rule which prohibited fishing on grassy patches. But before he could find and quote the specific prohibition (dated 1798) which, translated, read, "There shall be no fishing allowed from hotel windows or in the immediate vicinity of towers with pointy tops," Little Albert had snared the coat on the bent nail and, with one mighty heave, lifted it from its resting place.

However, Little Albert jerked the pole so hard in his attempt to retrieve it, that the coat went flying over their heads and way, way back toward the Eiffel Tower where it landed in the middle of a group of Japanese tourists who were all taking photographs of each other for the thirty-second time that day. Thinking the coat was a curious French kite (since it had a rope trailing behind) they all began to take pictures of it to show their friends back home. Then, one of the younger members of the party decided to fly it, to the delight of his friends who wanted something else to take pictures of as they still had seven or eight rolls of film left (and every Japanese tourist is required by law to use up ten rolls of film a day when on vacation – except for children under the age of five who haven't learned to hold a camera steady and sumo wrestlers for reasons which are unknown), but as soon as he got it going, by running with it very fast down the pebbled path, it got caught in one of the trees which lines the way. And shrugging it off as a poor French design, the party of tourists went on its merry way to the Place Pigalle leaving Fat Al, Little Albert, Henry-the-Nose and Anna staring up at the tree in dismay.

"Don't just stand there gawking!," said Fat Al to Little Albert, " Climb that tree and bring it back down!"

Unfortunately, the tree was in the middle of a very small circle of grass and as Little Albert readied himself for the ascent, he noticed the gendarme at his side, tapping his foot and shaking his head.

"I suppose we'll have to fish it down," said Fat Al.

But this time the gendarme was prepared and pointed to the 1798 law in his rule book which forbade fishing in the vicinity of pointy towers. (None of them could read it, of course, since it was written in French, but they got the message when the gendarme took their fishing pole away and cracked it over his knee, thus infuriating the owner of the crepe stand who had been looking all over for the pole that kept his awning up since without it he was forced to do business with a piece of canvas flapping in his face.)

So Fat Al, Little Albert, Henry-the-Nose and Anna just stood there looking up at the coat in the tree and wondering how in the world they were going to get it down.

"It's stuck up there for good!" said Little Albert.

"We'll have to wait till there's an earthquake or something to shake it down!" said Fat Al.

"But why do you want the coat so badly anyway? After all, it's my coat. And I certainly don't believe that silly story of yours that it was stolen and you had to take it back to London as evidence. In the first place, you're not policemen, and in the second place, who would ever come to Paris to trace a coat stolen from the Salvation Army! I might be young but I'm not stupid! I watch television, you know!" said Anna, all in one breath. "Anyway, I know how to get the coat down," she continued after taking a gulp of air, "but I'm not going to tell you unless you tell me why you want it so badly."

"If you tell 'er, tell me too," said Henry-the-Nose, who didn't know any more than Anna why they wanted the coat.

"Might as well," said Fat Al. "I don't know how to get it down. If she does, then we'll make her part of the gang and split the loot four ways instead of three. Agreed?"

Both Little Albert and Henry-the-Nose agreed. So Fat Al told the whole story – about how they had stolen the diamonds and then lost it because of Henry's sneeze. And how Anna's father had found it and how they had followed the family to their London hotel and then to

Paris. And how they had finally forced Mr Marple to tell how he had sewn the bag of jewels into the lining of his daughter's coat.

"I don't believe it," said Anna, when Fat Al had finished his story. "My daddy wouldn't do anything like that!"

"There's only one way to find out," said Fat Al. "Tell us how to get the coat down so we can check the lining and see."

"It's simple," said Anna. "I'm surprised you didn't think of it yourselves. It's your secret weapon."

"Our secret weapon?" said Henry-the-Nose. "Yer mean we 'ave a secret weapon?"

"Yep," said Anna. "Only it's not so secret. It's just that you've never used it to your advantage before."

"Well tell us what it is!" the gang of three all said together.

"Better still, I'll show you," said Anna. And this is what she did:

She took Henry-the-Nose by the hand and had him face the tree. Then she whispered something in his ear. And after he nodded back, meaning he understood her instructions, she took a leaf and began to tickle his nose. She tickled and tickled and Henry-the-Nose puffed up his cheeks and rolled his eyes until he couldn't stand it any more and just at that moment Anna shouted, "NOW!"

And at the word, Henry-the-Nose let forth a mighty sneeze, even mightier than the one on top of the Eiffel Tower. It was a sneeze of such velocity and power that it was heard by a little boy in Trieste, Italy who was eating a dinner of fried zucchini (which he hated) and wooshed it right off his plate and into his mother's face which made him laugh and thus earned him an early bedtime for the rest of the week. But back in Paris, Henry's sneeze did its job. Not only did it release the coat from the clutches of the tree, but it also shook off every leaf for miles around. And any stray object that had found its way into a Paris tree was shaken down by this mighty blast of air – old tyres, pussy cats, gym shoes, umbrellas, soufflé dishes (which had been thrown there by angry cooks whose soufflé had fallen), even an old four poster bed which had been placed there by a clochard who used it as a country home

– all this rained down on the city of Paris after Henry-the-Nose's sneeze.

And the coat? The coat went way, way high in the air – as high as the Tower itself – stayed a moment as if it were enjoying the view and then slowly drifted back down into Anna's arms.

"I've got it!" shouted Anna with glee. And she held it out triumphantly.

But, as she proudly displayed it to her new friends (remember, she had been made a member of the gang), the gendarme who had been watching these goings-on with growing suspicion, which, by nature of his profession, meant trouble, began walking toward Anna with a very serious look on his face, said something in French which was understood by all concerned to mean "I'll take that coat, if you please." (Though, in fact, the proper translation should have been, "Let me see your passport, identity card and letter of credit from your local café.")

"Blimey!" shouted Little Albert. "Here's another one who wants to nick our loot!"

"Let's run!" shouted Fat Al!

And the four of them started running, very quickly, away from the Eiffel Tower and toward the River Seine, with Little Albert in the lead, followed by Henry-the-Nose, Anna and Fat Al, who was huffing and puffing like a great steam engine going up a steep hill, while chasing them, close behind, waving his baton, his cape flying in the breeze, was the gendarme.

Fishing
for Host
INTERDIT
DE FAIRE
LA PÊCHE
A PROXI-
MITE
DES TOURS
DEFENSE
DE FOULER
LA PELOUSE

Chapter Thirteen

THE GENDARME, WHO was bigger and faster than any of the gang, would have definitely caught up with them if it weren't for the lady from New York who had been searching for her little Pekinese ever since it had run away from the Hotel de Paris when the gang had made their ridiculous entrance and Henry-the-Nose had sneezed, scaring the doggy out of its wits. As it was, she waved down the gendarme just before he was about to follow the gang across the busy boulevard which led to the promenade along the Seine to ask directions to the dog pound.

Being a gentleman, the gendarme stopped and took out his map of Paris to show her the way. But it was so complicated, that by the time he was done, the gang had disappeared down the stone steps which led to the river and, one by one, had jumped onto a long, narrow barge which was sailing slowly, quite close to the bank.

Fat Al, Little Albert, Henry-the-Nose and Anna, remained on the barge (which was carrying a load of pâté de fois gras to a small restaurant in Fontainebleau) hiding under the tarpaulin till they reached Île de la Cité (which is the little island where the Cathedral of Notre Dame stands) and the river split in two. Then, as the barge glided by a pleasant little park along the Right Bank, opposite the island and overlooking the Cathedral, they jumped off again.

There, as they huddled under a shade tree, Anna took her coat and began to rip out the lining of old wigs until, lo and behold, she found a little velvet bag which, indeed, had been sewn inside. And taking it out, she undid the ribbon and unloosened the tie cord and then she poured out the contents into Fat Al's cupped hands.

"Blimey!" said Little Albert seeing the sparkling gems falling like crystal rain drops as Anna poured them from the bag.

"Oh! Look at 'em shine!" said Henry-the-Nose as the glistening rays of afternoon sun bounced off the icy face of the diamonds, refracting all the brilliant hues of the rainbow and setting off a miniature light show in Fat Al's hands. "They don't look so dirty to me!"

"Dirty or not," said Fat Al, "they'll bring us a fortune!"

And sitting there beneath the beautiful shade tree, under the Paris sky, on the banks of the River Seine, overlooking the Cathedral of Notre Dame, the four of them continued to gaze at the precious stones in quiet wonder until Henry-the-Nose said, "Oi! Do we 'ave to sell 'em, mates?"

Little Albert added, "Couldn't we keep them for a little while?"

But Fat Al said, "It's no good being a robber if you can't even afford a decent plate of fish and chips!"

And Anna, who until then hadn't said a word because she was so amazed that her father had actually sewn the bag of jewels into her coat without asking her permission, said, "Yes, let's sell them so I can have enough money to run away from home for ever and ever!"

"Do you think we'll get enough for 'em to buy some proper musical instruments?" asked Henry-the-Nose.

"Certainly," said Fat Al.

"And enough for me to live on a farm and have chickens and cows and enough candy so I'll never go hungry?" asked Anna.

"Maybe," said Fat Al.

And for a while they all sat there, on the bench, dreaming their own special dreams. Then Fat Al opened up the last can of beans and the four of them dipped in and feasted on the succulent tomatoey goo. And when they had all eaten their fill and were quite satisfied, Anna joined Fat Al, Little Albert and Henry-the-Nose in a spontaneous song entitled "The Streets of Paris", while they watched the sun slowly sink in the wondrous Parisian sky.

"This is the best day in my whole, entire life," said Anna as she gazed upon the Cathedral now lit up in a golden hue.

"It's the best day in all our entire lives," said Fat Al, as he brought out the bottle of orange squash. "Here's a toast to our gang and to all our dreams come true!"

And all of them repeated: "To all our dreams come true!"

"Well, then," said Anna, after they had finished their drink. "Where do we go to sell our loot?"

"Little Albert's arranged all that," said Fat Al.

"Me?" said Little Albert. "I thought you did! You're the leader, you know!"

"That's right," said Fat Al. "And leaders have other people do things for them. They wouldn't be leaders if they did everything themselves!"

"That's not fair!" said Anna. "That's like having slaves!"

"An 'at's what 'e treats us like, sometimes!" said Henry-the-Nose.

"Well, I don't like it!" said Anna putting her hands on her hips and staring at Fat Al in a challenging manner.

"Do you have any ideas then?" asked Fat Al in a "so there" sort of voice. He knew from experience that some people might get angry at the way he ran his gang, but when put on the spot they didn't know how to run a loony gang of hopeless jewel thieves any better than he did.

But Anna, being a spunky little girl, did have an idea. "I guess we need a real authority. Someone who knows about selling things that don't rightfully belong to them."

"Do you know anyone like that in Paris?" asked Fat Al.

Anna nodded her head and sighed. "Yes," she said, "my father. After all, he smuggled the diamonds into France. And knowing my father, he wouldn't have done that without a reason. And the only reason I can think of is that he planned to sell them here."

"Good thinking," said Fat Al. "I'm glad we made you a member of our gang!"

"Me, too!" said Little Albert.

"Me, three!" said Henry-the-Nose.

So the four of them set off, back to the Eiffel Tower. And when they got there, they wisely took the elevator to the second level and then sneaked through the door that led up, up, up to almost the top, right below the needle where Anna's father was still tied to the rail which stopped people from falling over the side.

In the hours he had been tied there, Mr Marple had been trying to decide how on earth a sensible, well-respected factory owner, who wished nothing more out of life than to become a simple millionaire – how someone like him could have ended up tied to the top of the Eiffel Tower. So far, he had come to no definite conclusions, except to surmise that he should have stayed at home. For it now seemed to him, after all these cold, hungry hours, that he probably would be left up there forever or, at least, till the cleaning person decided to dust the needle, which could be who-knew-when.

So, Mr Marple was obviously very happy to see the gang, along with his daughter, Anna. And, if he hadn't been gagged and tied, he would have welcomed them back with open arms.

"I guess you've met my new friends, Daddy," said Anna, when they had all made themselves comfortable on the platform.

Mr Marple nodded his head and made a muffled sound through the empty carton of fish sticks Fat Al had used as a gag.

"We were wondering if you could help us out?" she went on. "You see, Fat Al, Little Albert, Henry-the-Nose and me, want to know how to sell our stolen diamonds and we were thinking that maybe you had some connections."

"Right," said Fat Al. "Just a word in our ear. It won't go any further, mind you. We'll even cut you in for a share of the take."

Mr Marple mumbled something that sounded like "ummfff, fumfumii!"

"Did you understand what he said?" Fat Al asked Anna. "I've always had trouble with American accents, myself."

"I think we better un-gag him," said Anna.

So Little Albert went over to Mr Marple and did just that.

"Thank you," said Mr Marple, as the ropes and gag were removed. "I was getting a little stiff in that position."

"We're sorry," said Fat Al. "We would have come back sooner, but we were very busy."

"It's just that my wife, Mrs Marple, will be worried about me and our daughter," said Mr Marple. "She tends to worry, you see, if we don't meet her on time.

And right now," he said, checking his watch, "we're over eight hours and twenty-three minutes late."

"Don't worry," said Fat Al, in an understanding way, "I'm certain she's waiting patiently at the Hotel de Paris for your return. But about our question – can you help us out?"

"Certainly," he said, "but first, could we please go down? You see, the truth is that I'm quite afraid of heights and this has been a most disturbing experience for me."

So they all walked down the spiral staircase, going round and round, down and down, until they reached the bottom. But as soon as they walked out of the Tower and set their feet on solid ground, Mr Marple suddenly yelled, "Help! Police!" to three gendarmes who were standing by the exit. "Arrest these men! They are the infamous jewel thieves who have stolen the diamonds from Her Majesty, The Queen of England!"

The gendarmes, of course, didn't understand a word of English. But one of them was the very same policeman who had chased the gang when they had run away with Anna's coat and he had brought two friends to help him search for them. So, regardless of the language difficulties, they were only too happy to take Fat Al, Little Albert and Henry-the-Nose each by the scruff of the neck and march them to a waiting police van which then drove them off to jail, leaving an astonished Anna crying, "But Daddy! They're my friends!"

Chapter Fourteen

THE MARPLE FAMILY was invited back to England by the Queen, herself, because of Mr Marple's help in recovering her precious jewels.

Fat Al, Little Albert and Henry-the-Nose were also returned to England, but for quite a different reason. The Queen was very angry at them and had them locked up in her jail.

The Marples, on the other hand, were invited to have tea at the Queen's Palace in appreciation of their assistance in getting the diamonds safely back where they belonged – that is in the bottom drawer on the left hand side of jewel cabinet number thirty-three in Treasure Room five hundred and seventy-nine in the third sub-basement of Buckingham Palace. But Anna, stubborn as usual, refused to go.

"I don't want to have tea with the old witch!" she said, folding her hands and turning blue in the face.

"It's not nice to turn down an invitation from her Royal Highness, the Queen of England," said Mr

Marple. "Besides, it's our chance to sell a few tea cosies."

"You go then," said Anna. "I'll have tea with someone else."

Mrs Marple was astonished. "Who would be better to have tea with than the Queen of England?" she asked.

"If you really want to know, I'll tell you," said Anna. And then she whispered something into her mother's ear.

"Really?" said Mrs Marple, with her mouth agape. "My, my!"

So it was arranged. While Mr and Mrs Marple were being entertained at Buckingham Palace, Anna had tea with Mary at Mary's Café and Diamond Cleaners.

Frankly, Anna couldn't have had a better tea if she had gone to Buckingham Palace. For Mary's tea was lavish indeed, with plates upon plates of sausages and mash and beans and fried eggs. It was a most splendid feast.

But it wasn't only the food that brought Anna to Mary's café. The truth was that Anna had a plan – and to put it into operation she needed Mary's help.

"It's not right, you know, that Fat Al, Little Albert and Henry-the-Nose have been sent to jail for ninety-nine years and ninety-nine days just for stealing the Queen's diamonds. After all, they weren't even cleaned yet!"

"Ninety-nine years and ninety-nine days?" said Mary in horror. "Just for nicking me sausages and a few dirty diamonds?" Mary being a fair-minded person was, of course, outraged. "That's ridiculous!" she said. "There must be something we could do!"

"There is," said Anna. And she told Mary the secret.

As soon as Mary heard what Anna had to say, she telephoned her friend, Lord Blimpy, whose diamonds she had often polished, and told him about the situation.

Lord Blimpy's first response was "Those scoundrels deserve a good head-chopping and then some!" But after Mary told him what Anna had said, namely that the gang possessed a secret weapon so formidable in power that England could once more rule the waves, Lord Blimpy's reaction was something else again.

"Besides the prestige," said Mary, "think of the balance of payments! Remember, the North Sea oil is bound to run out sooner or later."

Lord Blimpy phoned Lord Wimpy and Lord Wimpy phoned Lord Muck (the judge who sentenced the gang to ninety-nine years and ninety-nine days in jail and who had gone to Harrow, Oxford and the Island of Corfu the same year as Lord Wimpy).

"Don't you think you went a bit overboard, old chap?" said Lord Wimpy to Lord Muck. "I mean, ninety-nine years and ninety-nine days for a few diamonds. Blimpy tells me they hadn't even been cleaned!"

"Not cleaned?" responded Lord Muck. "I say! Why didn't that come out at the trial? I certainly never would have sentenced them to ninety-nine years and ninety-nine days if I had known that!"

"Well, Muck old boy, certainly a clever chap like you could think of something, what?" said Lord Wimpy with a sly chuckle. "After all, the North Sea oil isn't going to last forever, you know."

The gang's case was reheard the very next day. And this time, even though they again pleaded guilty, Lord

Muck imposed a sentence of six months in prison, suspended on the provision that Henry-the-Nose made himself immediately available to the Royal Air Force to test out the feasibility of using his sneeze in time of war.

That same day, Anna went back to Prairieview, Iowa with her parents, feeling that justice had been served. Mr and Mrs Marple also felt that justice was served, because Mr Marple went home with a treasure that was far greater than the diamonds he had almost gained.

"What is it?" asked Anna, when her father showed it to her on the plane ride home.

"It's something that will make our fortune in the tea cosy business," he said. "It is an emblem that will go on each of our packages so people will know that we are now making tea cosies 'By Appointment To Her Majesty, The Queen!' Mark my words, child," he said with a strange gleam in his eye, "we will make millions!"

But, somehow, that idea really didn't please Anna. And, curiously, though in succeeding years Mr Marple did become enormously wealthy because all through

America people were anxious to buy anything that was appointed by the Queen of England (since they didn't have a queen of their own to tell them what to buy), still Anna never felt quite as happy as she had been that day in Paris in the park on the banks of the Seine by the Cathedral of Notre Dame when Fat Al, Little Albert and Henry-the-Nose had made her part of the gang.

Chapter Fifteen

IF OUR STORY had ended here, it would have been quite a sad little tale. But, fortunately, it didn't. Because Anna, like all little girls got bigger and bigger and, finally, one day she found she was all grown up. And now that she was an independent person she decided to travel back to London on her own.

This time, however, instead of racing about, she spent many hours in the beautiful parks and walked very slowly and leisurely down the streets observing the people and all the wonderful sights there were to see, if one only took the trouble to see them. She fed the ducks in Serpentine Lake. She dipped her feet in the fountain at Trafalgar Square. She spent an entire day in the British Museum. And she went to concerts, plays and the cinema.

But one day when she was walking in the tunnel that led from Leicester Square to the Piccadilly tube line, she heard a song that sounded very familiar to her.

And walking a little faster, she soon observed three men playing a strange assortment of instruments – the one who was making a little dinging sound on a metal triangle was fat and smoked a cheap cigar; the one who was playing an old beat-up banjo was quite short and wore a cloth cap which fell over his eyes; and the one who was playing a used bicycle horn was tall and thin, wore thick glasses and had a great, big, throbbing, red nose.

When Anna ran up to them, they gave her a wonderful greeting. For, sure enough, the strange-looking men who were playing the funny-looking instruments were the members of her old gang.

That night they had a marvellous reunion at Mary's Café and Diamond Cleaners where they downed thirty-one sausages and eighteen bottles of vintage orange squash. And after they were finished eating and talking about old times, Fat Al told Anna how things hadn't been the same since she had gone, while Little Albert and Henry-the-Nose nodded their heads.

And Anna, in turn, told them how much she had looked forward to seeing them again someday.

Then, Henry-the-Nose said, "Oi! Why don't yer join our gang again?"

"Yeah," said Fat Al, who was growing tired of leading a gang of ageing nitwits for so long, "You can even be the boss."

"I can?" said Anna, very pleased to have been offered the position. "That's terrific, because I have a marvellous idea!"

"Tell us!" said Fat Al, Little Albert and Henry-the-Nose in unison.

Anna smiled and motioned for them to move close. Then, when they were near enough for her to whisper, she told them all the wonderful and exciting things they were going to do.

I wonder what it was, don't you?

The Gang